The Summer of the *Marco Polo*

To Maddy Lion—with oodles of love.
L.M.

ᘓᘔ

Acknowledgments

This story has been adapted from *The Selected Journals of L. M. Montgomery, Volumes I and II*, edited by Mary Rubio and Elizabeth Waterston, Oxford University Press (1985 and 1987).

Permission to adapt material from *The Selected Journals of L. M. Montgomery*, author of *Anne of Green Gables*, has been granted by Mary Rubio, Elizabeth Waterston and the University of Guelph, courtesy of the L. M. Montgomery Collection Archives and Special Collections, University of Guelph Library, with the approval of the heirs of L. M. Montgomery.

"ANNE OF GREEN GABLES" is a trademark and a Canadian official mark of the Anne of Green Gables Licensing Authority Inc., which is owned by the heirs of L. M. Montgomery and the Province of Prince Edward Island and located in Charlottetown, Prince Edward Island.

Text copyright © 2007 Lynn Manuel

Illustrations copyright © 2007 Kasia Charko

Library and Archives Canada Cataloguing in Publication

Manuel, Lynn

The Summer of the *Marco Polo* / written by Lynn Manuel; illustrated by Kasia Charko.

ISBN-13: 978-1-55143-330-1

ISBN-10: 1-55143-330-3

1. *Marco Polo* (Ship)–Juvenile fiction. 2. Montgomery, L. M. (Lucy Maud), 1874-1942–Juvenile fiction. 3. Shipwrecks–Prince Edward Island–Juvenile fiction. I. Charko, Kasia, 1949- II. Title.

PS8576.A57S84 2007   jC813'.54   C2006-906071-1

Summary: The wreck of a great sailing ship inspires a budding author, L.M. Montgomery.

First published in the United States 2007

Library of Congress Control Number: 2006937028

Orca Book Publishers gratefully acknowledges the support for its publishing programs provided by the following agencies: the Government of Canada through the Book Publishing Industry Development Program and the Canada Council for the Arts, and the Province of British Columbia through the BC Arts Council and the Book Publishing Tax Credit.

Orca Book Publishers
PO Box 5626 Stn. B
Victoria, BC Canada
V8R 6S4

Orca Book Publishers
PO Box 468
Custer, WA USA
98240-0468

Book design by Doug McCaffry.
Interior and cover artwork created using watercolors and pencil crayons.
Color Separations: ScanLab, Victoria, British Columbia.

Printed and bound in Hong Kong
10 09 08 07 • 4 3 2 1

The Summer of the *Marco Polo*

Written by Lynn Manuel · Illustrated by Kasia Charko

ORCA BOOK PUBLISHERS

I was only eight years old that summer, but I remember it as if it were yesterday. We were in school when we heard the great crash. It had been storming in Cavendish for days, yet we could still hear the crash through the wind. The Nelson boys said it was a tree blown down, and we all looked out at the old spruce woods. But I knew it wasn't a tree. The crash had a faraway sound. We would never hear a tree falling from so far away.

After school the Nelson boys and I hurried down to the shore where all the neighbors had gathered. With eyes as big as owls', we stared out at a great, black ship stranded among the breakers.

Grandpa Macneill was telling Mrs. Wyand all about it. "I was riding home," he said, "when I happened to look out to sea. I could hardly believe my eyes! A great sailing ship was heading straight for shore. When it hit a sandbar, the crew cut the rigging and the huge masts went over."

One of the masts was made of iron. That was the crash we heard a mile away.

Everyone on the shore was going wild trying to warn the crew to stay put. They would drown for sure if they tried to make it to shore with the sea raging. Some of the neighbors held up a board with the words *STICK TO THE SHIP AT ALL HAZARDS* painted on it.

The captain and crew were stranded out there all night. It was pitchy dark, and the wind was shrieking. I knew the poor men must be nearly chilled stiff. I couldn't keep the tears back, so I went to bed before Grandma saw me.

"Stop sniffling, Maud. You'll have something to cry for someday!" That's what she would have said. You can be sure of it.

I snuggled down among the blankets and had a good sob that night. How I wished there were someone to hold my hand! Someone to whisper words of comfort! If only Mother had lived.

In the morning a boat went out and brought the twenty men to shore—tired and wet and hungry. Captain Bull came to stay with us. The rest of the crew found boarding all around Cavendish.

Grandma and Grandpa Macneill have never liked to go visiting. And they don't care for callers dropping by for a cup of tea or a piece of cake, either. The post office is in our house, so the neighbors stop by to pick up their mail. But if Grandfather were not the postmaster, hardly anybody would ever come over. And that is the plain truth of it.

But it was different the summer of the *Marco Polo*. There were always droves of people at our house then.

Captain Bull was a fine gentleman, and I liked him splendidly. He was from Christiana, but he spoke English. Sometimes he got his words mixed up. I never laughed at him though. (My soul burns within me when people laugh at me for using big words.) The captain told us that the great ship stranded off our shore was the *Marco Polo*. She was once the fastest sailing ship in all the world! Then she got old and began to rot away. They were on their way to England with a cargo of timber when it began to storm. The *Marco Polo* sprang a leak. She became so waterlogged that the captain had to run her aground to save the crew and the cargo.

One evening I was sitting out front, scribbling away on the stone steps. (I have always loved to spin stories.) Our old dog, Gyp, was sleeping in the garden, curled up amongst the blue flowers and the lacy waves of caraway.

Of course I was missing Father. I often imagined that a Land of Lost Sunsets lay just beyond that purple strip of land that sticks out into the sea, and that one day Father and I would go there and share all our lost sunsets together.

I was deep in thought when Captain Bull appeared. We sat together in the dusky light and listened to the rustling of the leaves coming from the poplars. It sounded like distant surf, and I heard the captain sigh. He looked so forlorn. I knew he missed his great ship, just as I missed dear Father.

We had a good long chat about the *Marco Polo* that evening. Captain Bull told me the great ship was built in Saint John, New Brunswick. The men had trouble getting her into the water. When she finally went down the slip, the tide was going out and she landed nose-down in the mud. When they dug her out, the keel was twisted. The captain said that was the secret to her speed—a twisted keel!

The *Marco Polo* made her first trip to England in fifteen days, beating all the records. Then she raced other ships to Australia. When she won, they hung a banner from her masts that said *THE FASTEST SAILING SHIP IN THE WORLD*.

I showed the captain the jug Great-grandmother Woolner brought with her to Canada, filled with jam made from black currants, from her English garden. (We keep it on the top shelf of the china cabinet in the sitting room.) Then I told him the story of Harriet Kemp and her sailor.

The sailor was in love with Great-grandmother Woolner's sister, Harriet. On his last voyage, he had a jug specially made for Harriet. The sailor drowned but they sent the jug to Harriet anyway. She didn't like it, so she gave it to her sister, Great-grandmother Woolner.

The jug has a crack in it. You can see Great-grandmother Woolner's thumbprint in the white lead where she mended it. That's what makes the jug so dear to me—Great-grandmother's thumbprint in the white lead.

Pensie and I went berrying one day, and we picked our jars full in Sam Wyand's field. On the way home we saw the crew crowded into a truck wagon, bellowing out songs. We hitched a ride home with them along the old red road. Oh, how that day shines in my memory! Well and Dave ran behind us, trying to hang on to the wheels to keep them from turning. We had no end of fun!

When the captain finally paid off his men, the round mahogany table in our parlor was covered with gold sovereigns. Well and Dave and I couldn't stop staring. We sat outside on the grass under the parlor window while the crew fed biscuits to Gyp.

After a while, the captain came out. He took my hand in his and said, "I will always remember your kindness against me."

I knew he meant, "I will always remember your kindness to me." But I didn't laugh.

Then he added, "You have left your thumbprint on my heart, Miss Maud."

The *Marco Polo* was sold to a wrecking firm. When the captain and the crew left Cavendish, the great ship was still stranded off our shore. The cargo was swollen with moisture, and the wreckers had to cut through the ship's beams to get it out.

An auction was held in our barns for the cargo and parts of the ship. Everyone wanted a souvenir from the *Marco Polo*, and the bidding lasted all day. They spread a big sail on the ground in the barnyard and piled it with hardtack. It's a very peculiar kind of biscuit because it's as hard as rock, but it has a sweet taste. Dave was the first to try it. He got a bit off and chewed with all his might. He scrunched his face up every which way. My jaws ached from chewing all day!

I counted stars the night the wreckers stayed on board the *Marco Polo*.
It was the kind of storm that comes up all of a sudden. By the next
morning the sea was raging worse than when the *Marco Polo* ran
aground. We were all afraid the great ship would be torn apart by the
storm—with the men still on board! Three of the men tried to make it
to shore, but their boat got swamped by the waves. Two of them made
it back to the *Marco Polo*, but the third man drowned before our eyes.
Pensie and I could not let go of each other, we were so sick with terror.
Then the *Marco Polo* split apart and disappeared beneath the sea. The
wreckers were left clinging to a bit of the bow that was still held by the
anchors. People ran every which way, crying out with horror.

The neighbors tried to reach the men, but the sea was too wild. The
boats kept filling with water, and they had to return. Finally they dragged
a seine-boat all the way from New London Harbor with horses and lashed
empty barrels to the sides. (The sides of the boat, not the horses.) They
turned it into a lifeboat, and by evening the men were rescued.

The last of the *Marco Polo* disappeared into the sea with the next storm. The shore was piled with planks and wreckage for miles. I made wildflowers into a wreath and tossed it upon the waves with an armful of ferns.

"Pleasant dreams and sweet repose, dear ship," I whispered. "I hope you sail again on the seas of heaven!"

When I bent to touch the little waves, I felt the chill of the sea.

Three years have passed since the summer of the *Marco Polo*.
Everyone in Cavendish has claimed a bit of the ship that washed
ashore. George R. Macneill has the name-board on one of his barns—
now everyone calls him Marco-Polo George. And two gateposts made
from the pitch pine of her masts stand in our own barnyard.
   The *Marco Polo* has left her thumbprint on Cavendish.

Glossary

Christiana	Former name of Oslo, capital of Norway.
Hull	The frame of a ship.
Keel	Timber or plate extending along the bottom center of a ship.
Mast	A long pole set upright from the deck of a ship to support the rigging.
Rigging	Lines and chains used to work the sails and support the masts.
Seine-boat	A boat that employs nets for fishing.
Slip	A sloping ramp extending out into the water.
Sovereign	A gold coin.

Author's Note

When clipper ships carried passengers to Australia during the gold rush, the *Marco Polo*, launched in Saint John in 1851, had a worldwide reputation for being the fastest ship of the line. This created a great demand for vessels built in what is now the Canadian province of New Brunswick. Later, steamships replaced sailing ships in the passenger trade, and the *Marco Polo* was used to transport cargo between Quebec and Liverpool.

Lucy Maud Montgomery was a young girl in 1883 when the *Marco Polo* ran aground off the shores of Prince Edward Island. Maud was living in Cavendish with her grandparents, Alexander and Lucy Macneill. Her mother had died when she was just a baby, and her father had gone out west to work. Although the notebook diaries she kept from the age of nine to fourteen no longer exist, later journals written by the renowned author of *Anne of Green Gables* contain remembrances of childhood and of her Cavendish home. These remembrances from *The Selected Journals of L. M. Montgomery, Volumes I and II* have been adapted to recreate what happened that summer of the *Marco Polo*.